JACK CIANCIO

Job v. God

A Pleading in God's Court

Oh, that I knew where I might find him,
That I might come even to his dwelling!
I would lay my case before him,
And fill my mouth with arguments,
I would learn what he would answer me,

And understand what he would say to me.
Even now, in fact, my witness is in heaven,
And he that vouches for me is on high,
Hear now my reasoning,
And listen to the pleadings of my lips.

Job

Contents

Acknowledgments

I would like to thank the following for their contribution to this work.

Frank Levering, author and playwright, for his early assessment and encouragement.

Stephen Delacroix, retired epistemology teacher, for his review, suggestions, and catching those errors that escaped this writer's eye.

And wife Jane for her review and opinion from a general reader's perspective.

1

Introduction

In the Hebrew Bible the book of Job, along with Proverbs, Psalms, Ecclesiastes, and Song of Songs, falls under the major canonical category of Kethuvim or Ketuvim (writings).[1] Although there are many other books included in the Ketuvim, these five books, in both the Jewish and Christian canon, comprise the sub-category of sapiential, that is, wisdom, books of the Bible. The Christian canon also includes the Wisdom of Solomon and Ecclesiasticus. While the order may vary, Job, Proverbs, Ecclesiastes, and Psalms, which is mostly prayer oriented but still considered part of wisdom literature, are usually grouped together. Interestingly, the pleas for deliverance from enemies and recovery from grave illness found in Psalms 4–7 are quite similar to Job's pleas throughout his book. Psalm 8:4, "[W]hat are human beings that you are mindful of them, mortals that you care for them?" is nearly identical to Job's question in the book of Job 7:17–18.

Wisdom, obviously, is the main focus of wisdom literature, which begs the question, "What is wisdom?" Granted, the term is vague. In Scripture, however, it can be narrowed down. Two of the books of wisdom tell us directly that wisdom means "Fear of the Lord." Right from the start Proverbs says, "The fear of the Lord is the beginning of knowledge; fools despise wisdom and

---

[1] The Jewish Study Bible, 1275.

instruction" (1:7). In chapter 28 of Job, the interlude where wisdom is found, at verse 28 we read, "And he said to humankind, truly, the fear of the Lord, that is wisdom; and to depart from evil is understanding" (another instance of a copied psalm—111:10). It is further alluded to in Psalms and Ecclesiastes. "[B]ut the Lord takes pleasure in those who fear him," is found in Psalm 147:11. Ecclesiastes ends with, "The end of the matter, all has been heard. Fear God, and keep his commandments, for that is the whole duty of everyone" (12:13). Fear of the Lord as a chief component of wisdom is the principal theme of biblical wisdom literature and a prominent thread woven throughout the book of Job.

Consider the two meanings of fear. First is the obvious—fright, terror, the dread that something bad is going to happen to you. In Scripture it can also mean reverent awe, as in beholding with the utmost worshipful respect the unimaginable and formidable glory and power of God. Job experiences both. He reveals his terror when he declares *"If he would take his rod away from me, and not let his dread of him terrify me, then I would speak without fear of him"* (9:34-35). Additionally, he is keenly aware of the Almighty's awesomeness, *"I know that you can do all things, and that no purpose of yours can be thwarted. . . .Therefore I have uttered what I did not understand, things too wonderful for me, which I did not know"* (42:2-3). The irony of Job is that, while he is the protagonist in a major book of biblical wisdom literature, he is not wise. Good and righteous, yes; wise? not so much. Maimonides (1135–1204 CE), the great medieval Jewish rabbi and theologian, points out "wisdom is not ascribed to Job."[2] If he were wise, perhaps he would have better understood his plight and God's role in it.

The Book of Job—A Summary

For those who have not read the book of Job, or perhaps it has been some time since others have, a general summary might be helpful. The author

---

[2] Maimonides, *Guide for the Perplexed*, 3:22.

of Job is unknown. Although some early biblical language is evident, it is mostly composed of post-exilic language, which would place its time of composition around 539–332 BCE.[3] Ancient to modern scholars disagree on whether or not this is a fictional or factual story. Maimonides holds more to the fictional classification but a fiction unlike other fictions, for Job "includes ideas and great mysteries, removes great doubts, and reveals the most important truths."[4] It certainly lends itself to a more metaphorical and allegorical interpretation than literal, with its purpose being to explain "the different opinions which people hold on Divine Providence."[5] Fictional or not, Job represents all humans— frail, limited in comprehension, susceptible to misfortune as well as to emotional and physical pain; fearful of the "great unknown," and whose faith is not only often tested but also often conflicted. Job responds to his anguishing losses in typical human stages of grief— anger, bargaining, depression, and, finally, acceptance. Perhaps "exhausted submission" is more accurate than acceptance because Job's final capitulation seems to come rather easily after his prolonged and bitter protests over what he is convinced are God's unjust punishments.

Throughout the narrative we see glimpses of Job's recognition that he is engaging in a fight he cannot win: *Though I am innocent, my own mouth would condemn me; though I am blameless, he would prove me perverse* (9:20). He recognizes God's overwhelming might, *He is wise in heart, and mighty in strength—who has resisted him, and succeeded?* (9:4). He even foresees the end of his own story: *For he crushes me with a tempest* (9:17). In the end, rather than answer Job's simple question of why he, a blameless and righteous God-fearer, was targeted for affliction, God uses a whirlwind to overwhelm Job with his magnificent divine resumé. If he knows this is a losing battle, then why engage in the fight? Job is trapped between the futility of confronting God and the truth of his innocence. *See, he will kill me; I have no hope, but I will defend my*

---

[3] The Jewish Study Bible, 1502.

[4] Maimonides, *Guide*, 3:22.

[5] Maimonides, *Guide*, 3:22.

ways to his face. This will be my salvation (13:15–16), *I am not what I am thought to be* (9:35). Job is obsessed with an anguished sense of betrayal driven by his conflicted fear and love of a God who has suddenly turned a loving eye into what can only be taken as misdirected wrathful retribution. Job's motivating question is very simple, "Why me, Lord?"

The story begins with a prose narrative where Satan (Hebrew: *ha-satan*, "Adversary"[6] or "Accuser" in some versions) slips into a gathering of heavenly beings before God. When God asks him where he has been, Satan answers that he has been traipsing around earth. God asks if he has noticed his good and righteous servant Job. Satan points out that Job is only good and righteous because God has protected him and blessed him with a large family and prosperous business. God takes that as a challenge and allows Satan to take away all of Job's earthly possessions, including his children (but he is not allowed to physically harm Job), confident Job will still remain faithful. Satan agrees to the proposal. Job loses all, and sits grief-stricken and bewildered as to why this happened—but still faithful. God points out Job's abiding faith to Satan who challenges God a second time, this time asking to be allowed to physically torment Job, betting Job's faith in God would then collapse. God allows him to do so on condition he not endanger Job's life. For a second time God allows what Satan has proposed. This time Satan torments Job with agonizing boils and other bodily ailments. Again, Job sits in shocked bewilderment, not understanding why this would happen to him, a faithful and obedient servant of the Lord. Still, his faith in God remains firm.

At this point three friends—Bildar, Zofar, and Eliphaz—come to sit "shiva," that is, sit in silent mourning with their suffering friend. They sit silently for a week. When they do start to talk the book switches from prose to a poetic format in alternating dialogues between Job and his friends. Job and his friends all agree only God has the power to control Job's fate, and such punishment is only meted out to those who have sinned. God does not make mistakes, so it

---

[6] The Jewish Study Bible, 1502.

must be the victim's fault. Each friend tries to convince Job such misfortunes would only be visited upon him as punishment for some offense against God. Even Job's wife tells him to blaspheme God and get it over with. But Job sees the false premise in their argument—it is true God does not make mistakes, but Job knows, too, that he has remained righteous; he has not sinned; he has taken care of those in need; he has been, and will continue to be, faithful to God. Therefore, if his misfortunes are not due to his transgressions then there must be another reason. Why is he being punished? The three friends eventually give up trying to change Job's mind when a fourth friend—Elihu—shows up and not only takes up where the other three friends left off but chides the three of them for giving up. He then takes up the same line of attack: Job's misfortunes are God's punishment for his sins. The point of these four friends is that God does not make mistakes, and punishments and misfortunes happen only to the sinful. Job, knowing he has always been a faithful and righteous servant of the Lord, insists they are wrong, some mistake has been made, and if he could have his day in court he could prove them wrong and defend his good name, declaring, *"I would lay my case before him, and fill my mouth with arguments, I would learn what he would answer me, and understand what he would say to me."* (23:4–5). In addition to his personal anguish, Job is driven by the need to know why terrible things happen to good people (like him), while many of the sinful live happily and untouched by misfortune. *"Why do the wicked live on, reach old age, and grow mighty in power?"* (21:7), he asks.

God finally responds to Job in a whirlwind, pummeling him with all sorts of questions about what he knows of the creation, the workings of the universe, the nature of the cosmos—things that only God knows. Although God doesn't answer Job's main question, "Why me?" he does vindicate Job and Job comes to accept the unfathomable nature of God as being a mystery beyond humankind's ability to comprehend.

The Jewish Study Bible considers Job to be the most difficult book of the Bible to interpret,[7] due, in part, to its elaborate and poetic, albeit often ambiguous, language. Maimonides considered it the most perplexing book of the Bible.[8] With those two esteemed assessments in mind, any attempt to interpret it again would be rather quixotic. And yet, in spite of all the perplexity and ambiguity the book of Job has a story to tell. Just what that story is has been debated for ages. We know the details: God sets Job up as a target for Satan to torment so as to break his faith in God; Job loses his family, his fortune, and suffers unrelenting physical torment. Job's resulting frustration arises from the dissonant emotions resulting from his righteous love of God and the anger that comes from knowing he is mistakenly being punished by the very God he loves. "*I am blameless: I do not know myself* " (9:21), he cries! Rather than give in to his anger and blaspheme the Lord, Job simply wants to know "why?" *I will say to God, do not condemn me, let me know why you contend against me* (10:2); *Why have you made me your target?* (7:20). Therein lies the allure of this enigmatic story. Who hasn't, after misfortune has befallen them, especially after the loss of a loved one, felt a divine target on their back and questioned (perhaps cursed), God's plan and doubted his love? We all hold an opinion on how divine providence *should* work and when it doesn't we want answers, answers to which we presume we are entitled. What makes the book of Job so challenging is not just its perplexity but also its menacing tone. "Fear of God" does not exactly engender warm welcoming love. Once we really comprehend Job's angst, we subconsciously recognize that we are Job. Like the Sword of Damocles, God's judgment hangs over us constantly. Deep in our hearts we feel Job's terror, his fear of the Lord, knowing, blameless or not, his misfortunes could very easily be our misfortunes.

If you have ever experienced physical pain or emotional despair, the pain of loss, of grief, or depression, did you ever ask, "Why me?" Did you ever imagine what it would be like to stand before God and ask for an answer? The irony is, while most of us in such situations would like an answer, we would also be too

---

[7] The Jewish Study Bible, 1500.

[8] Maimonides, *Guide*, 3:22

terrified to stand and question God directly, knowing God would have a few questions for us that we probably would prefer not to have to answer. Such is Job's conundrum.

Job makes several requests to be given a trial so that he may be vindicated by what he knows to be true—that he is an innocent victim, he has not sinned, *for I know I am not what I am thought to be* (9:35). All of Job's requests are denied. If God will not take him to court, imagine if it were made possible for Job to take God to court, not out of anger or vindictiveness, but to find out why God contends against him and to prove his innocence to the world. Obviously, God cannot be guilty of wrongdoing, but Job believes a trial would give him a chance to prove his innocence and allow him to give voice to his suffering.

What follows is a creative account of how such a court proceeding might transpire. It is written as a trial recording (formatted similar to U.S. Supreme Court transcripts), but with more direct questions, answers, testimony, verbal confrontations and challenges. The segmented chapters in the book of Job allow for details of each perspective argument to get lost, whereas here the direct person-to-person dialogue expressing a particular viewpoint confronted by immediate interruptions and challenges raises tensions and passions that a straightforward essay or prose would lack. Actually, such a narrative would simply get in the way. Traditionally such narratives discuss the book of Job as a whole, while this book theorizes not only what Job's point of view might have been but also speculates on details of his and, by association, our humanity, which are glossed over in the biblical account and many theological expositions of the book. Arguably, the book of Job's renowned difficulty may be due to attempts to intellectualize its meaning rather than simply becoming immersed in Job's humanity.

The reader will find what might be called "stage directions" throughout to help set the scene and keep the proceedings flowing, but it is the dialogue itself that allows us to hear Job's story. Much of the dialogue is, of course, made up but dialogue in *italics* is taken straight from the book of Job (NRSV), edited only as needed to fit the context of the conversation. Each section taken or referenced from Job is followed by the numerical chapter and verse. Any other scriptural reference will also include the biblical book of reference. Finally, in hopes of adding some reality to the trial, there are descriptions of the characters as this author perceives them. The ambiguity of the book of Job seemingly invites readers to provide their own perceptions of how those characters would appear and act, therefore readers are encouraged to provide their own descriptions.

The book of Job opens with: *"There was once a man in the land of Uz whose name was Job"* (1:1). A plain and simple statement at first glance, but Maimonides provides a deeper explanation. He tells us that, the term *Uz*, can be used as a first name, as in Genesis 22:21, "Uz, the firstborn." Maimonides further informs us that, "It may also be the imperative of the verb, uz, 'to take advice,' or *uzu*, 'to take counsel,' as in Isaiah 7:10. In short, the name Uz expresses the exhortation to consider well this lesson, study it, grasp its ideas, and comprehend them, in order to see which is the right view."[9] Readers are now encouraged to consider well what might have been Job's side of this intriguing story and to come to a verdict of just what is the "right view."

* * *

------

9 Maimonides, *Guide*, 3:22

2

Job Speaks Out the of the Darkness

Let the day perish in which I was born. Let that day be darkness! Why did I not die at birth, come forth from the womb and expire? Now I would be lying down and quiet; I would be asleep; then I would be at rest (3:11–13). *Or why was I not buried like a stillborn child, like an infant that never sees the light?* (3:16).

As for me, I would seek God, and to God I would commit my cause (5:8). But how can a mortal be just before God? If one wished to contend with him, one could not answer him once in a thousand. Who has resisted him and succeeded? (9:2:4). *For He is not a mortal, as I am, that I might answer him, that we should come to trial together. There is no umpire between us who might lay his hand on us both. If he would take his rod away from me, and not let dread of him terrify me, then I would speak without fear of him, for I know I am not what I am thought to be* (9:32–35).

Unbearable pain torments each waking hour, and nightmares tear at my soul in sleep. Even there I cannot escape his judgment, even there I cannot escape his voice, for *God speaks in one way and in two, though people do not perceive it, in a dream, in a vision of the night, when deep sleep falls on mortals, while they slumber on their beds, then he opens their ears, and terrifies them with warnings that he may turn them aside from their deeds, and keep them from pride* (33:14–17).

JOB V. GOD

* * *

3

In the Matter of Job v. God

In The Supreme Court of Heaven

Job,
  Petitioner,
  v.
  God,
  Respondent.

The above-entitled matter came on for oral argument before the Supreme
Court of Heaven

* * *

Appearances

JOB: The petitioner. A man of slight build, dressed in faded blue jeans, a not-so-white shirt, black tie, topped by a vertically striped robe. Usually keeps his head down. A normally passive individual, but his misfortunes have made him a barely controlled emotional volcano.

BAILIFF: Dressed in a plain uniform
    RAPHAEL: Archangel of Divine Healing, presiding judge.
    RAGUEL: Archangel of Divine Harmony, associate judge.
    URIEL: Archangel of Divine Wisdom, associate judge
    RAMIEL: Archangel of Hope. Counsel on behalf of the petitioner.
    MICHAEL: Archangel. Divine Defender, Leader of the Army of God. Counsel on behalf of the respondent.
    All Archangels are dressed in gray robes with large hoods hiding their faces and long sleeves covering their hands. They move silently as if gliding rather than walking. Curiously, some hear their voices as male, others as female.

SATAN (aka Adversary, Accuser) appears as a human being. Well-dressed in a stylish suit; displays an arrogant, foppish manner—and a constant smirk. Evil is at home in his eyes.
    ELIPHAZ the Temanite: Friend of Job.
    BILDAD the Shuhite: Friend of Job.
    ZOPHAR the Naamathite: Friend of Job.
    ELIHU, son of Barachel the Buzite: Friend of Job.

Other names for God: Adonai (Lord), and El Shaddai (Almighty God).

Proceedings

(Job finds himself in a room both strange and yet somewhat familiar. Most of it is well-lit except for one small patch of shadow. Behind the long bench at the front of the room are three regally adorned chairs. That bench faces two others, one on each side of the room with a robed figure seated at each bench. A man in plain uniform approaches a bewildered Job and escorts him to a seat beside the robed figure seated at the bench on the left. Job sits down and the robed figure leans over and speaks softly to him. Their muffled conversation is suddenly interrupted by the man in uniform.)

BAILIFF: Alleluia, alleluia, alleluia. All rise. (The judges, their faces obscured by the hoods of their robes, enter led by Uriel, then Raphael, then Raguel and take their seats.) This special court, appointed and permitted by El Shadai is now in session. The venerable Raphael, Archangel of Almighty God, presiding.

RAPHAEL (gavels the court into session): Be seated. Who appears before this solemn court?

RAMIEL (stands and bows): Ramiel, Archangel of the Lord, appears for the petitioner Job, Your Honor.

MICHAEL (stands but, as leader of God's army, he neither bows [except to El Shadai], nor does he acknowledge the title of "honor" normally afforded judges): Michael, Archangel and Leader of the Army of God, for the respondent Almighty God.

RAPHAEL: Very well. The bailiff will read the matter brought before the court.

BAILIFF: Petitioner Job seeks redress of grievances and is suing respondent, Almighty God, for breach of promise and purposefully, and knowingly conspiring to create a hostile living environment, defamation of character, physical and emotional trauma, and loss of property. All lower courts having passed on this matter, it is now referred to this special court convened with the permission of the Almighty, the respondent, who wishes these matters to be resolved and finally laid to rest. To that end, the respondent temporarily and voluntarily relinquishes all omnipotent and omniscient powers, divine threat, and hostility and allows petitioner Job to freely, without fear of retribution, state his case. He further appoints Raphael, Archangel of Divine Healing, as presiding judge; Raguel, Archangel of Divine Harmony; and Uriel, Archangel of Divine Wisdom, as associate judges.

—Oral Argument Of Archangel Ramiel on Behalf Of The Petitioner—

RAPHAEL: *Anyone who argues with God must respond* (40:2); therefore, we will hear arguments today in the matter of Job v. God. Counsel for the petitioner, you may open.

RAMIEL (stands before the judges' bench and bows): Thank you, your most illustrious and righteous emissaries of El Shadai. And may it please the court. For the record it is neither petitioner's nor my intention to put the Almighty, himself, on trial. He is named respondent only as a matter of record because the created order has no primary movement other than as he allows. As such, petitioner seeks to address and ask to be granted two things of the Almighty: *Withdraw your hand far from me, and do not let dread of you terrify me, then call, and I will answer; or let me speak, and you reply to me* (13:20–22). The petitioner was a righteous and undeserving innocent victim of the outrageous pain and suffering that was inflicted upon his very being and life. He desires to affirm his righteous innocence to the world, thus revealing the injustice of the dreadful misfortunes that were visited upon him through an apparent conspiracy, the motives of which are, as yet, unknown. The emotional pain of those misfortunes still haunts him.

I speak, now, for the man called Job and you, no doubt, know some of the details of his story. Many know him in connection with the word "patience," as in, "The patience of Job." Patient? Yes, in that he remained steadfast in his loyalty to God; but impatient in the lack of a response to his repeated request for a just hearing. And why should he not be impatient? (21:4). Yes, he is that Job. But I am here to tell you he is so much more. Should it be the case that you do not know who he is or, perhaps, your memory needs refreshing, please allow me to chronicle the events that bring him and his cause before the court today.

Many millennia ago, he was a righteous, God-fearing, and innocent man; a son of the east, a farmer who, through arduous work and, yes, perhaps some divine favor—favor that, I might add, he earned—had achieved a fair and comfortable amount of riches and prosperity. He had many comforts of life. A much-treasured family of seven sons and three daughters whom he loved more than life itself. He lived in Uz where he had many friends and business associates. Although he was not a member of any of the Judean tribes, he was accepted by them as righteous and considered an honorable man, a man of integrity, a trustworthy man who not only dealt honestly and fairly with everyone but also came to the aid of many in distress.

RAPHAEL: You state these events occurred many millennia ago, which leads me to ask why has it taken him so long to seek redress for these alleged injuries?

JOB: That's a good question! One that I have been asking from the beginning. And, I might add, millions since then have asked the same question!

RAPHAEL (bangs gavel): The petitioner will maintain order and allow his legal representative to address the court on his behalf.

RAMIEL: My apologies, Your Honor. As you can imagine, bitter memories such as these evoke the most painful emotions in my client. To this day he sometimes feels he is still living through those agonizing terrors. In response to your question, Your Honor, the answer goes to the heart of this case. That petitioner brings this case should be a surprise to no one. As he suffered the outrageous and undeserved attacks upon his physical and emotional well-being, as he saw his loved and cherished family taken from him, as he incurred the insults of once trusted friends, as he suffered unbearable physical anguish, he frequently voiced his desire for legal recourse and a just hearing in an impartial court.

JOB: Yes, an "impartial" court. But God *will surely rebuke you if in secret you show partiality. Will not his majesty terrify you, and the dread of him fall upon you?* (13:10–11). *Let me have silence, and I will speak, and let come on me what may* (13:13). *I will say to God, Do not condemn me; let me know why you contend against me* (10:2). *Hear now my reasoning and listen to the pleadings of my lips* (13:6).

RAMIEL (raises a handless sleeve toward Job to settle him down and quickly responds as Raphael reaches for the gavel): Again, I apologize for my client's outburst, Your Honor. If I may continue. Moreover, other reasons prevail as to why it has taken so long to seek justice. First of all, for a thousand years of human time, there was no written record of what happened to him. All anyone knew of his plight before then was handed down by word of mouth. To bring his case before the court prior to the existence of an officially sanctioned written record would have been dismissed as hearsay.

The record to which I refer has come to be known as the book of Job, and is found in the most holy of books, the Bible, which, today, seems to be regarded by a substantial number of humans as an official document of divinely approved and motivated actions. *The* Word of God. Some say, undisputed; some insist it is a literal revelation of the thoughts, desires, and purposes of El Shadai himself. So that you might better understand the petitioner's position you must recognize that in his time the things that eventually came to be written down were known only through, well, gossip, to be frank. At this time, I would ask the court to stipulate for the record that the Bible and, by inclusion, the book of Job are a fair and accurate representation of the respondent's thinking on matters great and small. I cite a passage from this record. "The law of the Lord is perfect, reviving the soul, the decrees of the Lord are sure, making wise the simple" (Ps 19:7).

RAPHAEL: Let the record show the biblical account of the incident referred to in what is now called the book of Job is accurate and acceptable for the court to accept into evidence.

RAGUEL: Well, I think we have to be careful in making such a hasty generalization. I mean, we have to take into consideration that words and context had an entirely different meaning in the petitioner's lifetime than they do today, to say nothing of the fact the words of the created reflect nothing more than humanity's futile attempt to understand Shadai's glorious but incomprehensible thoughts. It has been noted that this holy book, "speaks in the language of [humans},"[10] not the Almighty. It is my understanding this book of Job has been overhauled frequently and has many variations. It has come to be considered by all people of the "Book" as the most perplexing story included therein. Its main point is obscure; even now we cannot be absolutely certain of its accuracy.

JOB: Why the hell don't we ask him? After all, he "inspired" it?

RAPHAEL (bangs gavel): Again, I must caution you, Mr. Job, to be silent and allow your counsel to speak for you. I would hate to have you removed from the court room.

URIEL: This Bible issue will loom large and will influence our thinking unless we arrive at an acceptable agreement as to just how we receive it. I move that the part known as the book of Job as written be considered as factual evidence, stipulating that if petitioner, who, after all, lived through those events has any information to the contrary, or offers clarification, that we allow him to bring such facts to the court's immediate attention for due consideration.

____

[10] Maimonides, *Guide*. 1:33.

RAGUEL: I agree to my venerable colleague's motion.

RAPHAEL: I have no objection. Do representative counsels agree?

RAMIEL (looks over at Job, who reluctantly nods his head): Counsel for the petitioner agrees, Your Honor.

MICHAEL (leaning back in his seat, seemingly disinterested): Yeah, sure, whatever . . . Uh, I mean, counsel for the respondent agrees.

RAPHAEL: Counsel may continue.

RAMIEL: It was said of petitioner Job that he had an even and gentle temperament, that he loved life, was happy, and felt blessed. He was known for following the commandments of the Lord his God to the letter of the Law. And yet on an arbitrary whim all that he had, all happiness, was taken away from him. We have evidence that he was a victim of a conspiracy between the respondent and the one known as Satan.

MICHAEL: I object to counsel's use of the words "conspiracy," "arbitrary," and "whim." Counsel has presented no evidence to support such allegations.

RAPHAEL: Sustained.

RAMIEL: Acknowledged, Your Honor. Please allow me a little leeway and I will soon show evidence to support those allegations.

URIEL: At any time, was petitioner given a guarantee that his life would be or should forever continue to be happy and comfortable?

RAMIEL: Well, uh, no, not directly, Your Honor, but, again, the Bible makes certain claims. I offer the following Scripture to be placed into evidence (hands a document to the bailiff, who shows it to Michael and then hands it to Raphael).

RAPHAEL (reviews the document and passes it to the other judges to review. They nod in agreement): The court has no objection.

MICHAEL: No objection.

RAMIEL (reads from the document): It is written by the prophet Jeremiah: "For surely I know the plans I have for you, says the Lord, plans for your welfare and not for harm, to give you a future with hope. Then when you call upon me and come and pray to me, I will hear you. When you search for me, you will find me, if you seek me with all your heart, I will let you find me, says the Lord" (Jer 29:11–14).

RAMIEL (sets the paper aside and continues): None of this was afforded to my client, Your Honors. And so, it seems by subsequent events that the Lord's plan did include harm, and hope was nowhere to be found. Petitioner's repeated prayers to be heard were answered with divine stillness. Then, Your Honors, he was handed over to this evil one, Satan, for torture.

SATAN (jumps up out of the shadow, shaking a scrawny finger at the judges): I object! Counsel's remark labeling me the "evil one" is slanderous. I am not on trial here—

RAPHAEL (cuts Satan off with a slam of the gavel): That you are not on trial remains to be seen. Your objection, however, is sustained. Be seated! Counsel will limit his presentation to facts in evidence.

JOB (comes out of his seat shouting): Wait a minute! He most certainly is on trial. He not only instigated the calamities that befell me, he's the one who prompted Shaddai to add to my miseries. He is a principal co-conspirator in this whole damn affair! He—

RAPHAEL (banging away with his gavel): Order! We will have order in the court! Mr. Job, I have warned you repeatedly to restrain yourself. You leave me no choice but to have you removed.

RAMIEL: If I may. Petitioner's emotional angst is quite understandable, perhaps—

JOB (slumps back into his chair): Indeed, Your Honor, indeed. Please forgive me. My soul is overburdened with anguish and my speech torn with passion. *O that my vexation were weighed, and all my calamity laid in the balances! For then it would be heavier than the sand of the sea; therefore, my words have been rash* (6:2–3).

RAGUEL: Perhaps under these circumstances we should allow the petitioner and his counsel time to confer—and calm down.

RAPHAEL (pauses to consider): Very well. Counsel, I will give you thirty minutes of human time with your client to bring him under control. This court is recessed for thirty minutes.

RAMIEL: Thank you, Your Honor.

BAILIFF: All rise. (Judges file out of the court room. Ramiel sits next to Job. They engage in a seemingly heated discussion. Although their discussion is mostly inaudible, Ramiel could be heard to frequently say, "No!" while shaking his head. Job likewise is quite animated, his arms flailing around. Finally, after a sustained pause in their discussion, Ramiel, his head down, nods. Court resumes.)

BAILIFF: All rise. This special hearing appointed and permitted by the Almighty Adonai, is back in session. The blessed Archangel Raphael presiding. (Judges re-enter and take their seats. Raphael gavels the court back into session)

RAPHAEL: Be seated. Counsel. have you resolved the problem with your client?

RAMIEL (standing again before the judges' bench): Well, in a manner of speaking, Your Honor. With the court's indulgence we ask that the petitioner be allowed to speak for himself. I know this is quite out of the ordinary but, considering my client's emotional state, I believe it to be the best way to get to the truth of the matter without interruption. Additionally, I offer that this is in keeping with the court's previous order to allow my client to directly challenge any facts he finds to be in error in the book of Job. My client agrees to respect and maintain the decorum of the court. While he can best relate the facts of this event and their personal consequences, I will continue as his legal advisor and respond to whatever legal challenges may arise.

RAPHAEL: Well, this is quite unheard of. Considering the serious nature of this proceeding I must, for the record, hear the petitioner's reasoning for this decision. Mr. Job, please approach the bench. (Job slowly approaches to stand beside Ramiel and bows before the judges.)

RAPHAEL: Sir, considering the profound nature of this trial, what is it you hope to gain by addressing the court directly rather than through your highly skilled and experienced counsel?

JOB: (Pauses to thoroughly consider his answer. His heart is pounding; his hands, held out in front of him in supplication, are shaking. His need to plead his case, however, overrides his normally timid tongue.)

Your Honor, I know that *if one wished to contend with him, one could not answer him once in a thousand* (9:3). Still, I beg you, *listen carefully to my words, and let my declaration be in your ears. I have indeed prepared my case, I know that I shall be vindicated* (13:17–18). I intend to show I was blameless, I was upright, and yet, not only was I not afforded his protection, as read earlier, but a conspiracy was perpetrated against me to destroy my cherished family and imperil my life with unrelenting physical torment. I know *if I speak, my pain is not assuaged, and if I forbear, how much of it leaves me?* (16:6).

(The judges pause and bow their heads toward one another. No speech is heard because divine spirits do not communicate in the manner of humans.)

RAPHAEL: Very well, petitioner will be allowed to address the court directly. (Ramiel returns to his seat.)

JOB: (Bows) Tha—thank you, Your Honor and most venerable associates. Please forgive me in advance for anything I say or do that is out of line with court procedure or might offend divine sensibilities. As a mere human I can only stand in awe of your presence and this opportunity that has been granted to me.

SATAN: Oh, please! Awe, indeed! Quit sucking up and just get on with it, man.

RAPHAEL: Silence! Job, please continue.

JOB (turns to face Satan): *Bear with me, and I will speak; then and after I have spoken, mock on* (21:3)—as is your nature. (Job glares at Satan for a moment before turning back to Raphael.) The indisputable facts are these, Your Honor. The Almighty singled me out to Satan as a prime example of his work. *"Have you considered my servant Job? There is no one like him on the earth, a blameless and upright man who fears God and turns away from evil"* (1:8), he said. I would like it noted for the record that the Almighty knew I was beyond reproach. "Blameless, upright, a shunner of evil," he said. Many came to convince me I was being punished for some transgression, to me known or unknown, but I am vindicated by the very words of the Almighty himself as written in the holy record. Satan had, indeed, has, no fear challenging the words of God, *"Does Job fear God for nothing? Have you not put a fence around him and his house and all that he has?"* (1:9–10), he asked. Then he directly challenged the Almighty: *But stretch out your hand now, and touch all that he has, and he will curse you to your face* (1:11). He was setting me up. Rather than considering my good fortune was due to my righteous love of God and my hard work, Satan challenged the Almighty to take away all I had, including my beloved family, all but my flesh and bones, alleging my fear of God would be as stout as dust in the wind! The Almighty's words meant nothing to this malicious fiend but, obviously, his words meant something to the Almighty who gave me over to him saying *"Very well, all that he has is in your power, only do not stretch out you hand against him"* (1:12). And so, the sovereign master of the universe allowed Satan, with a puff of his vile breath, to blow away all I held dear in life.

The record simply, callously, indicates I lost my family as if I lost my purse and a few cheap coins. But allow me to tell you a little about "those few coins," that is, my family. Benjamin, my firstborn son, had grown into a fine upright man with a family of his own. He had a keen intellect and was chiefly responsible for the growth and prosperity of our business. My third son, Osiah, was more the philosopher than businessman. He and I would often sit in the field at night gazing at the stars. Orion and Perseus were his friends, and he would tell me of his dreams to one day join them in the heavens. It brings me slight solace to believe the Almighty's game ended by granting him his youthful wish. And my daughter Remaya was with child. It would be her first. Not only was her life ended, but for some mysterious divine purpose, so was the life of the child she carried in her womb. I could go on. What transgression could be so heinous that justified the murder of those innocent souls, leaving me in endless grief? The Almighty's wrath against a sinner, even an alleged sinner such as I, comes loaded with collateral damage. No matter how precious my new family is to me, and they are, it does not relieve the agonizing loss of those first pillars of my life. *Even if it is true that I have erred, my error remains with me* (19:4), not with my family and certainly not with my many servants who were also killed! How can their destruction be justified? What did the Almighty gain by taking their lives?

In spite of all that, Your Honors, my faith remained unbroken. The evidence lives in the record: *In all this Job did not sin or charge God with wrongdoing* (1:22). But even that was not enough for these two puppet masters. No, not nearly enough! Seeing the wholesome flesh still left on my bones Satan wanted even that. Again, he challenged Shadai, *"Skin for skin! All that people have they will give to save their lives. But stretch out your hand now and touch his bone and his flesh, and he will curse you to your face"* (2:4−5). And again, the Almighty fell for his taunts and relinquished my body and my righteous spirit to Satan's second challenge, saying *"Very well, he is in your power; only spare his life"* (2:6). "Spare his life," he said. Spare his life! Spare my life for what? To win a bet with Satan? To prove his power? To watch a creature who loved him with whole heart, mind, and soul wreathe in agony and pain? (Job raises his eyes and his voice.) *If I sin, what do I do to you, you watcher of humanity? Why have you made me your target? Why have I become a burden to you? Why do you not pardon my transgression and take away my iniquity?* (7:20−21). (Job pauses with head down, silent except for a few sobs. He wipes his eyes and then softly continues.)

What good would living do me? *I loathe my life* (10:1). Why not simply kill me and let me lie in peaceful repose? Is death not enough for you or do you get some pleasure out of your divinely sanctioned torture? Are we truly your children or your puppets—playthings meant only to give you servile homage and endless entertainment?

RAMIEL (approaches Job and puts his cloaked arm around his shoulders): Your Honors, these facts are recorded in the Book of Truth. The petitioner and I now humbly welcome the court's questions.

URIEL: At any time did you directly seek an explanation from Shadai for the misfortunes visited upon you?

JOB: Most certainly I did, Your Honor. *I cried out to him, but he did not answer me; I stood and he merely looked at me. He turned cruel to me* (30:20−21). He continued to persecute me and harass me until my courage melted away. I pleaded in anguish and no one came; I cried out, no one answered. I prayed with heart and soul and every fiber of my being for an end to my afflictions and was ignored. All that I feared came upon me relentlessly. I found no ease, no quiet, no rest (3:25−26).

RAPHAEL: Job, forgive me, but I would like some clarification. Just what, exactly, motivates your pleading before this court?

JOB (faintly smiles before answering): Ahh, that's the question, Your Honor. The truth is, and I think you and Adonai would immediately know if it wasn't true, that my mind and my heart have been filled with all sorts of emotions. Sometimes even I am confused. I wonder if I have loved him or hated him more for the way he so violently wrenched my world apart and tortured my body and soul? Maybe I loved him too much not to hate him for the betrayal I felt in my heart. As a child of God, I worshiped and adored him, only to realize he was a father who all too easily offered this child up for torture. He *poured me out like milk and curdled me like cheese* (10:10). I was berated numerous times for not simply cursing Shadai and getting it over with. Even my foolish wife turned on me, encouraging me to "*curse God and die!*" (2:9). But this I did not do. "*Shall we receive the good at the hand of God, and not receive the bad?*" (2:10), I replied. I was obedient to the end. This court must know, must proclaim for eternity, that throughout these agonizing events I still honored and worshiped this Almighty, whose name we reverently withhold utterance. I never forgot that all any of us have comes as a blessing from above. *The Lord gave and the Lord has taken away* (1:21). I never took that for granted. Indeed, the record shows that for all that he put me through I *did not sin or charge God with wrongdoing* (1:22). Allow me, in closing, to say there is no doubt of my love of God, either before or after the miserable events to which I was subjected. You can check the record. And know, too, this God was chosen over Baal, over Marduk, over many other gods. We had choices, and we chose to worship this One.

URIEL: On the face of it, the record certainly implicates the Almighty's hand in the start of your misfortunes. Is it your contention that somehow he colluded with Satan to put you through the pain and suffering that you endured? Who do you think is at fault here?

JOB: Well, Your Honor, the record gives indisputable evidence and clearly indicates a conspiracy between the two to offer me up as a sacrifice. Shadai singled me out as an epitome of his good works. I was dangled like fish bait before Satan's rapacious jaws seeking a new soul. The record clearly shows the Lord yielded to Satan's challenge to prove my faith. Satan's motives are easy to understand, he serves only himself by serving up evil, pain, and misery. He merely lived up to his hideous nature and did what he does best. But this is what I do not understand and perhaps what goes to the very heart of my case: Why does the Almighty, being the Almighty, allow Satan the freedom to torment his supposedly beloved children? I would never allow a wolf to threaten any of my children who were keeping watch over my flock. There seems to be some well-hidden ulterior motive here.

SATAN: Again, outrageous slander! I need no allowances from your god (having no honor, Satan shows none), I rule independently and freely! I am the only one who can answer such questions. (Satan's outburst causes Job to flinch and Michael to turn quickly and take a step toward Satan.)

RAPHAEL (bangs his gavel several times): Order! Order! (Sternly). Michael, I will handle this! Satan, be quiet and be seated. It is obvious we will have to hear from you at some point. Until then, sit down and shut up! (Satan slumps back into his seat.)

MICHAEL (returns to his seat): Alright, I will wait my turn at this vile creature.

RAPHAEL: Enough! Do my associates have any further questions?

URIEL: Job, I understand Adonai sent you friends to offer solace and comfort during this entire sorrowful affair. Does that not show he had not abandoned you and wanted to bring you through these misfortunes intact of mind and spirit?

JOB: Oh, yes, my friends. *Miserable comforters all* (16:1)! Well, they were convinced my misfortunes could only be due to my great wickedness (22:5). They would not consider any other explanation. I examined my life in minute detail and could produce no offense on my part that would justify the horrendous losses imposed on me. The one thing upon which we all agreed, going back to your prior question, was that God was the cause of my suffering. Their persistent arguments against me only contributed to my misery. I feel *those who withhold kindness from a friend forsake the fear of the Almighty. My companions are treacherous like a torrent-bed* (6:14-15). (Job pauses and takes a deep breath.) No, in truth their hearts may have been in the right place; they were, after all, merely regurgitating what they had been taught about the Almighty and his ways. I might have talked as they did were I in their place (16:4). I knew what they did not, and so much more—I knew I was an innocent victim, mistakenly chosen as a target of the Almighty's ire. *I know I am not what I am thought to be* (9:35).

RAGUEL: Is it true you have been compensated for your distress with the restoration of a loving family and your fortune has been restored many times over?

JOB: I, I guess, yes, that is true, Your Honor, but—

RAGUEL: Is such compensation not satisfactory? Does it not absolve the Almighty and satisfy your need for further legal compensation?

RAMIEL: If I may, Your Honor, I will respond to that. Compensation or lack thereof is not the issue of these proceedings. Answering one way or another may influence the court's decision. As I presented in my opening remarks, petitioner brings this case to show first of all that he was an innocent victim of a conspiracy, to clear his name, and, if possible, to discover the reason he, a good and righteous fearer of the Lord, was targeted for misfortune. Subsequent compensation does not erase the pain of loss of his original family and should not be considered in deciding a just verdict.

RAPHAEL: Thank you, counsel. If there are no other questions we will now hear from counsel for the respondent.

—Oral Argument Of Archangel Michael On Behalf Of The Respondent—

MICHAEL (stands and approaches the judges' bench): Thank you. We have all heard an interesting tale of woe presented by the petitioner and his counsel. With all due respect, nothing has been presented that really necessitates a response from the respondent. That being said, I request an immediate dismissal of all charges.

(Ramiel quickly restrains Job who starts to come out of his seat. Unintelligible whispers are exchanged except Job can be heard to say, "What's he afraid of?" as he sits back down.)

RAPHAEL: On what grounds do you base your motion for a dismissal?

MICHAEL: Petitioner *opens his mouth in empty talk, he multiplies words without knowledge* (35:16). The very idea that God Almighty should answer for any of his actions or should be called to reveal his plan or in any way be held responsible for the end result, is absurd. *Can you find out the deep things of God? Can you find out the limit of the Almighty?* (11:7). Besides, as Raguel pointed out, and petitioner admits, he has been justly compensated for his misfortune. So says the Lord.

RAPHAEL: I would remind you that these proceedings were approved and divinely sanctioned to allow the petitioner to air his grievances; whatever answers that come to light from these proceedings are simply unanticipated consequences. As counsel for the respondent, you may withhold any information deemed divinely privileged. On the other hand, I again remind you that these proceedings have been divinely approved and as such you will provide in an honest and forthright manner whatever information is sought within the parameters as agreed upon. The issue of compensation has been noted and the statements of both you and the petitioner on that matter will be taken into consideration. Additionally, you will show proper respect for the authority of this court. Is that understood?

(As God's appointed judge in this trial, Raphael shows Michael no special deference; besides, even archangels are not immune to petty rivalry.)

MICHAEL: It is, as long as my request and reasons for dismissal are noted for the record.

(Job notices that there is always a pause before Michael speaks when all the archangels bow their heads as if they were attending to something beyond the human ear.)

RAPHAEL: Duly noted. You may begin your opening.

MICHAEL: As I was saying, petitioner presents a sad tale of misfortune and raises questions of who is to blame—God Almighty, Satan, both? Perhaps neither, *for misery does not come from the earth, nor does trouble sprout from the ground; but human beings are born to trouble just as sparks fly upward* (5:6). *God does great things and unsearchable, marvelous things without number* (5:9). (Turning toward Job, he adds), Bear in mind, also, *that he saves the needy from the sword of their mouth* (5:15). So says the Lord.

URIEL: If humans are born to trouble, does that mean they are unalterably destined for misfortune? Has Adonai so planned it for humanity? Do they have any means within their power to control their destiny, to escape their misery?

MICHAEL: Humanity can only understand the term "plan" as a time sequence. It is beyond humanity's comprehension to understand God's actions in equivalent terms; that is, God does not "plan," he just is. A concept beyond human understanding. As an eternal being who always was and always will be, time holds no such meaning. So says the Lord.

URIEL: I ask again, do humans have any way of controlling their destiny?

MICHAEL: El Shadai knows what humans are capable of, both good and bad, and gives them the means and knowledge to choose the path to the destiny of their choice. It is also true that at times someone else's choice or some random event may intersect that path causing a different outcome. El Shadai neither clears nor blocks the path to anyone's destiny. If, by chance, the resulting outcome is, from a human perspective, unfortunate then humans must deal with the unintended consequences. The Almighty "does not willingly afflict or grieve anyone" (Lam 3:33). He provides humans with ways to cope even if such coping mechanisms seem futile to them. So says the Lord.

RAPHAEL: Can humans not pray to the Almighty to assure an uninterrupted path, or perhaps to undo a crossed path, to get to the end they have chosen?

MICHAEL: No matter how many prayers humans make, the Almighty may choose not to hear (Isa 1:15). Even though they weep before the Lord, he still may not give them his attention (Deut 1:45; Jer 7:16). Humans have difficulty accepting that no answer is an answer. His silence can be as eloquent as words. Intercession and deliverance do not always follow each other. On the other hand, humans are often blind to the answer he does give or dislike what they think is his answer. They only pray for what they want—their will, not his, be done—thereby missing a divine opportunity. Prayers are conversations and all too often humans simply stop conversing and miss the wisdom and comfort that comes from a full and sincere heart-to-heart conversation with El Shadai. Humans seem to think that they are the initiators of these conversations and that God must respond. God can never be anything less than the initiator. In reality, there is that of God within each human that, if humans are open to listening, is the initiator and to which humans should respond. So says the Lord.

RAGUEL: We know that human comprehension is limited, but does it not appear to them that the Almighty's power can be ruthless?—Love me or else! And it seems in Job's case his righteous love could not save him from the "or else."

RAMIEL: Excuse my interruption, Your Honor, the point you just made goes to the heart of petitioner's case. You pose a question of great significance: Why do even the most righteous, the most loving of God's creatures, in this case Job, suffer outrageous and painful misfortunes while many vile creatures (Ramiel turns to cast a glance at Satan) live happy and unaffected lives?

MICHAEL: *Bear with me a little, and I will show you, for I have yet something to say on God's behalf* (36:2). To think that Almighty God would collude with this (waves his handless sleeve toward Satan), evil creature is beyond comprehension. God *does not despise any; he is mighty in strength of understanding. He does not keep the wicked alive, but gives the afflicted their right, he does not withdraw his eyes from the righteous* (36:5-7). So says the Lord.

JOB: Archangel Michael's words are comforting, indeed, Your Honors, but *how long will he torment me, and break me in pieces with words?* (19:1). *When I think of it I am dismayed, and shuddering seizes my flesh* (21:6). Murderers and adulterers go unpunished. Rich and powerful men know no limits of inflicting harm. *They thrust the needy off the road; the poor of the earth all hide themselves* (24:4). *From the city the dying groan, and the throat of the wounded cries for help, yet God pays no attention to their prayer* (24:12). *Why do the wicked live on, reach old age, and grow mighty in power?* (21:7). *Their houses are safe from fear, and no rod of God is upon them* (21:9).*They spend their days in prosperity and in peace they go down to Sheol. They say to God, "Leave us alone! We do not desire to know your ways. What is the almighty that we should serve him? And what profit do we get if we pray to him?"* (21:13-15). Indeed, what profit do any of us obtain from prayer? Such is the world in which human creatures live. I know my words fall on deaf ears. You accuse humans of being uncomprehending, but I can't help but wonder if what we lack in comprehension the divine realm lacks in compassion. *Have you not asked those who travel the roads, and do you not accept their testimony, that the wicked are spared in the day of calamity, and are rescued in the day of wrath?* (21:29-30).

MICHAEL: God's ways may seem strange to uncomprehending humans. But *where shall Wisdom be found? And where is the place of understanding? Mortals do not know the way to it, and it is not found in the land of the living* (28:12-13). *God understands the way to it, and he knows its place. For he looks to the ends of the earth and sees everything under the heavens* (28:23-24). It is a paradox of *how happy is the one whom God reproves, therefore do not despise the discipline of the Almighty. For he wounds, but he binds up; he strikes, but his hands heal* (5:17–18; Ps 147:3). So says the Lord.

JOB: Yes, and he can just as easily kill as he can heal; God speaks, "If you want my mercy, then let me gain the victory over you; if you want my goodness, then let me take your life." What choice do we have? All praise the Holy Father God—or not! No matter what we sow, he chooses what we reap.

RAPHAEL: We seem to be straying from protocol here. Michael, your motion to have this case dismissed has been denied. Now, let's address the heart of the petitioner's case: Did respondent El Shadai collude with Satan and purposefully and knowingly conspire to create for petitioner a hostile living environment resulting in defamation of character, physical and emotional trauma, and loss of property?

MICHAEL: Very well, I need no prolonged summation. To think that this good great God would collude with this (pauses and waves an arm in Satan's direction) fiend is hardly worth a response.

JOB: Wait, excuse my interruption, Your Honor. If it is hardly worth a response, then why put me through such atrocities? What did he want of me? He knew me to be blameless, and yet his anger was unrelenting. *Though I am innocent, I cannot answer him. I must appeal for mercy to my accuser* (9:15). But the record clearly shows a conspiracy between El Shadai and Satan to offer me up as a sacrificial lamb for the Almighty to prove he can garner eternal love where Satan cannot. My innocence meant nothing. I implore you not to let the bitterness of my words discount the validity of my complaint—

MICHAEL: *You who tear yourself in your anger—shall the earth be forsaken because of you, or the rock removed out of its place?* (18:4).

JOB (shaking his bowed head): My anger, O' Mighty One? My anger is long spent, long since swallowed by sorrow and despair.

RAGUEL: Sorrow for whom? Yourself?

JOB: For myself, yes, Your Honor. I have earned a bit of self-pity. But sorrow also for the fact that this magnificent God finds it necessary to relate to us in such a hidden and secretive manner. *What are human beings, that he makes so much of them, that he sets his mind on them, visits them every morning, tests them every moment?* (7:17–18; Ps 8:4). It is almost as if he fears us; fears that if we knew some truth we would no longer have need of him; fears that if we get too close we might dare tear off the mask and accidentally scratch the divine face. The record shows that when humans get too close he will do all he can to confound them (Gen 11:5–8). Was that Adam's sin? Perhaps the forbidden fruit was a piece of the divine consciousness that Shadai could not abide sharing, so—

RAPHAEL: Job, considering your plight and the fact that this is a specially convened heavenly court, I have allowed you some leeway in taking your testimony to the edge of blasphemy. I would, however, caution you to walk that edge ever so carefully.

JOB: I fear Your Honor mistakes my true devotion for hypocrisy. I assure you I hold the face in much higher regard than I do the mask. I do not fear that I blaspheme because heaven sees my heart and knows what I say. I will not be a slave to those purple-robed sages of form who dwell on the incomprehensibility of God and yet presume to make him comprehensible according to their telling. Humans work within limited bounds of reason, but it is God-given reason, and I will use what I have to reverently seek what answers he may provide. How may any of us ever see the light if we choose to remain in the dark or thoughtlessly place our faith in those whose chest-thumping righteousness amounts to no more than polishing a golden calf?

RAPHAEL: Understood but heed my words of caution. You may continue.

JOB: Thank you. Well, let me finish along those lines by pointing out that he avoids our most pressing questions and instead swamps us with his glorious resumé and overwhelms us with questions the answers to which he hides from us and then taunts us as too unworthy to know. In the end we are left only to shudder in timid submission, reduced to forlorn comfort in the hope that by submissively offering more love we may save ourselves from his wrath. Forgive me for being such a lowly uncomprehending child, as Michael so disdainfully puts it, but I wonder if such love is born more out of a broth of intimidation than love-affriming reverence. What kind of love is it that is nourished by the fear of his terrifying power and the dread of him who can at any time exchange whatever meager earthly happiness we have achieved in life for unwarranted pain and suffering? Michael consistently points out the incomprehensibility of humans, but it seems that does not apply to Adam—

MICHAEL: Objection! What occurred between El Shaddai and Adam is irrelevant to this case.

RAPHAEL: Sustained. Job, please confine your remarks to your situation only.

RAMIEL: Your Honor, if you please. For the record I would like to point out Job's reference to Adam is relevant in regards to this concept of human incomprehension, and since Michael raised this issue it is, therefore, a permissible line of testimony. It goes to the question that if humans are uncomprehending, and Adam, being made from clay, was human, then how can he be held responsible for understanding this whole concept of good and evil? We in the angelic realm are not even privy to the thoughts of Shadai's mind. We know that *God puts no trust even in his holy ones, and the heavens are not clean in his sight. In his servants he puts no trust, and his angels he charges with error,* so how much more can be expected of humans? (4:18; 15:14–16).

MICHAEL: Adam and his partner were told by God himself what was and was not permissible, but they still disobeyed and listened to Satan. Fools despise wisdom and instruction (Prov 1:7). So says the Lord.

URIELL: Michael, there is a difference between being foolish and uninformed. Did Shadai ever explain Satan's evil intent to Adam or the consequences of following his prodding?

MICHAEL: The court earlier put into the record that I am allowed to withhold certain divinely privileged information and I do so now. So says the Lord.

RAPHAEL: Michael's last objection is sustained, but I will allow Ramiel's statement to remain in the record for future discussion. Job, you may continue.

JOB: I will, as you direct, focus on my situation. The question I was getting to regarding Adam and Eve, and that my esteemed counsel clarified, was whether or not we can ascribe their sin to their uncomprehending divinely-created nature? They were denied knowledge of pain, of want, of deprivation, of loss, of agony, or grief. They knew no alternative measure for understanding what love means. Satan was behind their disobedience, but in my case there was no disobedience. I was blameless, the Lord God said so. The only connecting link is Satan. But what does it matter? It seems we are all born either Jacobs or Esaus—never knowing whether the Almighty loves us or hates us.

Your Honor, the record shows that throughout my horrific tribulations I never blasphemed God or accused him of wrongdoing. I am grateful to this special court for giving me a chance to raise questions that might seem as challenges to the divine mind. If I stepped over the line, I apologize. (Job bows his head as an uncomfortable silence falls over the courtroom.)

RAPHAEL: I think this would be a suitable time for a brief recess. Court will resume in fifteen minutes.

(Fifteen minutes later the bailiff calls the court to order.)

RAPHAEL: Well, since it seems we have deviated from normal court procedure we may as well continue. At this time, I will allow Satan to address the court.

SATAN: (Approaches the judges' bench, his dark eyes seeming to absorb rather than reflect the light. He does not bow but, unlike Michael, it is a snub born of contempt rather than hierarchical equality.) Well, I never thought Michael and I would ever agree on anything, but this case proves the exception. I also move to have this case dismissed, and for much the same reason, which is that the petitioner has offered a pitiful tale of woe but without substantial proof that I had, of my own volition, contributed to his misfortune.

RAPHAEL: Denied. Do you have anything else to offer?

SATAN (chuckling): Your denial is hardly surprising. In that case, allow me, the only one here who really knows what transpired between myself and your god to set the record straight. I had no knowledge of this man Job and his alleged righteousness until your god pointed him out to me. As far as I was concerned, he was simply one of millions of foolish creatures who submit to your god's needy, but confusing, demand for absolute adoration. So, I took him up on the challenge. If you consider him almighty, then you must know he could have stopped me anytime he wanted. Why didn't he? I would draw your attention to the record where it unequivocally states that I could not have done these atrocious things of which I am accused unless your god first stretched out his hand. And I followed his command not to take Job's life. The petitioner, likewise, could have stopped it anytime he wanted by simply acknowledging his pain and suffering were not worth the price of his professed and, I might add, misplaced fear of his god. It should have seemed obvious that Job's god betrayed his righteousness.

URIEL: Are you claiming you had no part in Job's misfortunes and torture?

SATAN: Well, (he clears his throat), no, not exactly. You see, it is all part of the eternal cosmic game between your god and me. I allow him to think he has power over me, and yet I am free to traipse about the world as I please, doing what I please. And, as the record shows, I can even insert myself into a gathering of his best and brightest.

URIEL: And when does this cosmic game end?

SATAN: Difficult to say. I guess when one of us has captured all the pawns. Unfortunately, they are a shifting bag of black and white; so, the game goes on.

RAGUEL: Doing as you please, huh? Why do you think that, despite all your various tortures, Job did not blaspheme his God, nor admit any wrongdoing, and held his life-long charitable behavior of helping those in need as behaviors for which he truly felt were worth suffering?

SATAN (examining his fingernails): Foolishness. I have dealt with a million creatures like him. Granted, this man, for whatever reason, held out better than most, but in the end, he will probably yield to my truth—most do. You see, it is not always the big misfortunes to which humans succumb that pave the way into my world but rather their numerous small petty misdeeds. I have found that the living soul is always up for grabs.

JOB: I think I alone can answer that question, Your Honor. Loyalty to El Shadai and caring for those in need gave my life meaning. I could always hold my head high knowing I served the Lord not only in my heart and soul but also with my words and deeds. I never flaunted my righteousness but simply lived it as proof of who I was and what I cared about. Foolish or not, I have always believed that no matter all the divine pitfalls, there is an eternally good truth to loving our neighbor. Humanity's problem is that it too often allows Satan to deceive us in mistaking our neighbor for an enemy.

RAPHAEL: Satan, if nothing else, we owe you some thanks for confirming the nature of your "truth." We should all take heed. You are dismissed.

SATAN: Ah, yes, truth, illusion. Illusion, truth. Now you see it, now you don't! One never knows, does one? Ever the master magician is your god. (Rather than return to his seat, Satan struts his way out of the court room, his bloodless lips now pulled tight into a mocking sneer.)

RAPHAEL: Before we go to closing arguments, the court needs to hear from Job's friends who maintained close contact with him throughout his ordeal. Eliphaz the Temanite, please come forward. My esteemed associate Uriel may begin the questioning.

(Eliphaz approaches the judges' bench, head down, and bows.)

URIEL: Eliphaz, from what we can gather from the record, you, Bildad, Zophar, and later Elihu gathered around and initially had some intense conversations with Job, is that correct?

ELIPHAZ: Yes, Your Honor.

URIEL: Could you please summarize your conversations with Job for us?

ELIPHAZ: Of course, Your Honor. Well, I started by commending Job for all he had done for others, but now that misfortune had befallen him he had become *impatient and dismayed.* I asked him if his *fear of God gave him confidence and the integrity of his ways,* that is, whether or not all the charitable deeds he had done *gave him hope (4:5-6)* that he would eventually be rewarded. It was obvious to me, well, really, all of us that God does not punish without reason, therefore, Job must have sinned at some point. I have always believed that *those who plow iniquity and sow trouble reap the same (4:8).* And isn't that exactly what we were seeing, that *by disease the skin is consumed, and the firstborn of Death consumes their limbs* (18:13).

URIEL: So, it was your position that God only punishes sinners, but with proper penance the sin is forgiven and some reward is eventually bestowed.

ELIPHAZ: Yes, Your Honor. Bildad followed up on the need for repentance, telling Job that *if he would make supplication to the Almighty, surely then he will rouse himself for him and restore to him his rightful place. Though his beginning was small, his later days will be great* (8:5–7). And, as we see, Your Honor, that is how everything turned out.

URIEL: But Job never did admit guilt and, although he finally repented for his lack of understanding God's actions, he never made any type of supplication for sinful behavior, did he?

ELIPHAZ: No, not that I know of.

URIEL: And yet his possessions were restored. So, your argument that God only punishes the wicked, but with supplication they may be restored to a rightful place, doesn't seem to be valid, does it?

ELIPHAZ: I, uh, I'm not sure I follow, Your Honor.

URIEL: Well, Job never admitted guilt for wrongdoing, nor did the Almighty accuse him of wrongdoing. In fact, the Almighty admitted that Job was a *blameless and upright man who fears God and turns away from evil* (1:8). Therefore, we may conclude Job was an innocent victim. And, although it is alleged that the Almighty played some role in Job's misfortune, in the end he lifted his hand and restored twofold all that Job had lost. So, it is as Job maintains, God *destroys both the blameless and the wicked* (9:22). In other words, misfortune falls on the innocent as well as the sinner. Is that not so?

ELIPHAZ: When you put it like that, I guess so. But, Your Honor, how do we know who is blameless? Only God would know that.

URIEL: And yet you and your friends presumed to know God's mind—Job had sinned and his misfortunes were proof of God's requisite punishment.

ELIPHAZ: We have been taught that punishment always falls on the wicked, while the righteous are spared. Such is God's way; such is God's justice. Such is our tradition.

URIEL: Perhaps you should reconsider that tradition in light of what happened to Job. According to the record you assumed Job was wicked (22:5), that he failed to listen to the counsel of God (15:8), assumed that you had more wisdom than he (15: 9-10), and condemned all mortals as being unable to be righteous (15:14). As a mortal you must be included in such condemnations and equally guilty of *limiting wisdom to yourself* (15:8) rather than to God. I yield to my associate, Raguel.

RAGUEL: I have no more questions for this witness. I call Bildad the Shuhite to testify. (Bildad approaches the judges' bench and bows.)

Bildad, were you involved in these conversations with Job?

BILDAD: Yes, I was, Your Honor.

RAGUEL: Please share with this court what transpired between you and Job.

BILDAD: Well, Your Honor, I tried to comfort Job by reminding him that if he was patient through these misfortunes and repented his sins, a great reward would eventually be bestowed on him, as you yourself put into the court record earlier, Your Honor. I added *God will not reject a blameless person nor take the hand of evildoers* (8:20). Job's family was destroyed, and we know the wicked *have no offspring or descendants among their people and no survivor where they used to live* (18:19). Job's misfortunes were evidence of guilt and relief could only be found in his repenting for his wickedness. I said to him that, *"if you seek God and make supplication to the Almighty, if you are pure and upright, surely then he will rouse himself for you and restore to you your rightful place, though your beginning was small, your latter days will be very great"* (8:5-7). And that is what happened.

RAGUEL: Earlier my associate Uriel challenged that assumption. Job never repented for a sin so egregious as to justify the enormity of his misfortunes and yet a family and fortune were restored to him. Therefore, your conclusion of God's reasoning for inflicting these misfortunes is erroneous. Is that not so?

BILDAD: Yes, I guess so, Your Honor. But I feel there is something missing. None of what you say seems to be supported by what our ancient sages taught or what we have come to know of God's justice, which is he punishes the wicked and protects the righteous.

RAGUEL: Thank you for your testimony. You are excused. I now call Zophar the Naamathite to testify. (Zophar approaches the judges' bench and bows.) You have heard Eliphaz's and Bildad's testimony. What can you add?

ZOPHAR: Your Honor, allow me to pick up where Bildad just left off, that is the wicked receive just retribution. It seemed to me there was a contradiction in Job's reasoning. He claimed his *conduct was pure, and he was clean in God's sight* (11:4), but God does not make mistakes. Actually, as bad as Job's punishments were, they probably should have been worse (11:1-12).

RAGUEL: How could you possibly know the extent, if any, of Job's guilt? Or the reasons for God's actions? Are you able to know the mind of God?

ZOPHAR: I know what I have been taught, and I know what I saw. As for the wicked, *the possessions of their house will be carried away, dragged off in the day of God's wrath. This is the portion of the wicked from God, the heritage decreed for them by God* (20:28–29). And that is what happened to Job. Therefore, his sin must have been great, and God's retribution justified.

RAGUEL: Is it possible God had some other motive for imposing such misfortune on Job?

ZOPHAR: No.

RAGUEL: Your confidence in your ability to know the mind of God is, in the least, interesting. You are excused.

RAPHAEL: I would like to finish this line of questioning by calling on Elihu son of Barachel the Buzite to testify before us.

(Elihu stands before the judges, but where the other friends kept their heads down, Elihu stands erect; the arrogance of his youth calming any apprehension of standing in front of these exalted judges; he is confident he can lay out a solid case against Job.)

RAPHAEL: Elihu, the record shows that not only were you the last to confront Job but also that you had a confrontation with Eliphaz, Bildad, and Zophar. Please tell the court the details of those discussions.

ELIHU: Your Honor, at first, out of respect for my elders, I sat in silence. I thought *let days speak and many years teach wisdom* (32:7). But when it became apparent to me that *it is not the old that are wise, nor the aged that understand what is right* (32:9), I had to speak up, for it is not age *but the breath of the Almighty that makes for understanding* (32:8). Of the three who had gone before *there was in fact no one that confuted Job, no one among them that answered his words* (32:12). They had simply given up, dismayed (32:15) by Job's unrelenting claim that he was innocent. I realized they were wrong in their approach and Job was just as wrong by insisting he was an innocent victim and somehow

God's allowing these misfortunes was a, uh, a divine mistake—as if that were possible! Reluctantly, Your Honor, I gave in to my anger at the failure of all four of them for failing to recognize God's justice.

RAPHAEL: Job's other friends present what looks like a comprehensive picture of the nature of Job's misfortunes. All three insisted Job had sinned, that his misfortunes were justified, and since God cannot make a mistake, Job must be guilty. Furthermore, Job's continuing to insist that he was innocent and his refusal to repent further alienated him from God's forgiving grace. Do you agree with that?

ELIHU: Yes, Your Honor.

RAPHAEL: Well, then, what made you think you had more to offer?

ELIHU: I felt their efforts did not go far enough and that *my words declared the uprightness of my heart and what my lips know they speak sincerely. The spirit of God has made me and the breath of the Almighty gives me life* (33:3–4). I have profound respect for Job. I stand before God no differently than he; I, too, was *formed from a piece of clay* (33:6). But Job could not see beyond his own innocence, "*I am clean, without transgression: I am pure, and there is no iniquity in me*" (33:9), he declared. He took his misfortunes as God's personal attack on him, *that God counted him his enemy and put his feet in the stocks* (33:10–11). He could not, would not, look beyond his own misfortune to consider God's actions to be part of an eternal cosmic plan much greater than the blink-of-an-eye moment of a creature's life. *For God speaks in one way, and in two, though people do not perceive it* (33:14). Therefore, we *mortals must fear him. He does not regard any who are wise in their own conceit* (37:24).

RAPHAEL: I want to make sure I have this straight. Job's misfortunes were divinely imposed justification for his wickedness; furthermore, you all concluded that Job was guilty of focusing on his own victimization rather than consider that his circumstance was part of El Shadai's incomprehensible grand plan for the cosmos. Is that correct so far?

ELIHU: Basically, correct Your Honor. I would say that Eliphaz, Bildar, and Zophar put more emphasis on Job's sinfulness, his need for repentance, and that his misfortunes were just consequences for his wickedness, while I focused more on his self-righteous indulgence of innocence which prevented him from acknowledging the incomprehensible mind of the Almighty, creator and manager of the entire cosmos.

RAPHAEL: But does that not make you guilty of the very thing for which you accuse Job?

ELIHU: How do you mean?

RAPHAEL: Well, if the mind of God is incomprehensible, then it should be as incomprehensible to you as to Job. And yet you, and the others, seem quite self-assured that God's actions were, without doubt, due to Job's wickedness. Is that not reading the mind of God? Is it not possible that there might be some other reason for God acting as he did?

ELIHU: We know God punishes sinners; Job was being punished; therefore he was a sinner.

RAPHAEL: Such thinking fails as a logical argument. You are taking the final consequence, "Job was a sinner," and then justifying it with unprovable premises.

ELIHU: We are a separate people, set apart by our religion and our Law. Such logical reasoning is a human abstract; accordingly, what might seem illogical to some, is made logical by our Law and our tradition.

RAPHAEL: And yet, God did not agree, is that not so? What was the final result of the various attacks of the four of you on Job?

ELIHU (finally bows his head, shuffles his feet, takes a long pause before answering): Uhm, well, uh, in the end the Almighty condemned us and we could only be forgiven by begging Job for forgiveness.

RAPHAEL: Interesting. And why did Shadai condemn you?

ELIHU: He spoke to Eliphaz, saying, "*My wrath is kindled against you and against your two friends; for you have not spoken of me what is right, as my servant Job has*" (42:7).

RAHAEL: In other words, Job was right and you four were wrong. Correct?

ELIHU: Yes, Your Honor.

RAPHAEL: What do you think God saw in Job's response to his misfortunes that was right and that you and the others were wrong?

ELIHU: In truth, Your Honor, I am not sure and am still trying to figure it out. Although I was not directly condemned by God, I paid heed to his words. I begged Job's forgiveness. I also asked the Almighty to enlighten my mind, for these matters are quite perplexing. There is obviously something in my faith that I am missing.

RAPHAEL: While I commend your faith and adherence to tradition, I urge you to examine your religious convictions more closely to determine whether or not they are truly in line with the Lord's and that you are not simply "wise in your own conceit." Thank you for your testimony. Job, would you like to respond to the testimony of your friends before we go to closing arguments?

JOB: Although I find it difficult to believe anyone would rush to make the decision to annul my testimony, I know from other evidence how great is the power of my misfortune when combined with the ignorance of my opponents; thus, I think I have a reason to be skeptical about the high prudence and holiness of those in whom the final decision depends, for they may be in part deceived by this fraud which is going around under the cloak of zealous faith.

—Closing Arguments—

RAPHAEL: The court will now hear the respondent's closing argument. Michael.

MICHAEL: I say to Job, *Will you even put God in the wrong? Will you condemn him that you may be justified* (40:8). *Have you listened in the council of God? And do you limit wisdom to yourself?* (15:8). *Who has put wisdom in the inward parts, or given understanding to the mind?* (38:36). Do not think God does not understand your pain. It has already been noted God speaks in various ways and people are not often capable of perceiving it. El Shadai presented you with a host of wonderments—*Have you comprehended the expanse of the earth? Declare, if you know all this. Where is the way to the dwelling of light, and where is the place of darkness?* (38:18–19)—these are beyond your knowledge or even your ability to think about. The strength of humans and the earth are nothing compared to that of God. But Job, know this: By remaining faithful you have shown how firmly you believe in the truth of God's word, and how well you have comprehended the true essence of God; you have proven that you cannot be misled by the Adversary to corrupt your faith in the Almighty. From your actions, for which you deserve to be truly called a God-fearing man, all people shall learn how far they must go in the fear of God.[11] The Lord has spoken.

RAPHAEL: The court will now hear the petitioner's closing argument.

JOB: Thank you, Your Honor. Most Illustrious Michael, thank you for your kind and encouraging words. Please know I do not argue against God, I merely ask why he turned his hand against me. According to the record, he knew I was blameless; therefore, his contending against me left me utterly dismayed.

---

[11] Maimonides, *Guide*, 3:24; (see also, Gen 22:12).

What was I to think? What was I to do? My cherished family taken from me, my business destroyed, my very life threatened by unimaginable physical torments. Everything had been surrendered up and only one thing was left to me—my life—and I was determined to hold on to it. Is that so wrong? My hand that thought it had found firm support in my love of God reached into an empty nothingness. And yet there are those who condemn me for not looking beyond my mortal peril to some greater good. I felt trapped in an inescapable, never-ending nightmare. I suspected God had led me to the summit of an abyss and as I stood there terrified by the height I heard God's challenge, "Now jump!" If I jumped, what was waiting for me? Could I be assured he would catch me? And if I didn't jump how else could I prove my faith? How would I ever learn to trust? In truth, I still don't know. But now I am ready to lay the matter to rest. *I know that the Lord can do all things, and that no purpose of his can be thwarted.* I have come to know that *I have uttered what I did not understand, things too wonderful for me, which I did not know. I had heard of him by the hearing of the ear, but now my eye sees him, and I repent* (42:2–5) for my hesitation to believe.

RAMEL: Petitioner now rests his case, Your Honor.

(Job leans on Ramiel as they return to their bench. The associate judges bow their heads toward Raphael who, shortly after, signals he is ready to render a verdict. Ramiel and Job stand as Raphael gives the verdict.)

—Verdict—

RAPHAEL: Petitioner, in your opening statement you asked this court to rule on two things, first of which was a request of the Almighty God to *withdraw his hand far from you and not let dread of him terrify you.* It is obvious now by the return of a family of seven sons and three daughters, your health, and a business twice what you had that the Almighty has not only withdrawn his hand but also rewarded you handsomely for your continuing loyalty to him. Your second request, that he *call, and you will answer; or let you speak, and he reply to you* has been fulfilled by these court proceedings. El Shadai called, you answered, and you were afforded more than enough time to speak. I assure you that through this court Almighty God has heard you and has provided what answers he could that you are capable of understanding. Now, whether or not he still terrifies you is a condition that only you can come to terms within your heart. "The end of the matter, all has been heard. Fear God, and keep his commandments, for that is the whole duty of everyone" (Eccl 12:13). Such is our verdict in the matter of Job v. God. Court is dismissed. (With a bang of the gavel Raphael brings the court proceedings to an end.

The judges file out of the courtroom. Job, somewhat dismayed, falls back in his chair and drops his head into his hands. "If I won, what have I won? If I lost, what have I lost? Who is this God?—Who am I?" After a few minutes he raises his head, finds himself alone in his room, and hears Raphael's fading voice—)

<blockquote>

"For the Lord will not reject forever.
Although he causes grief, he will
have compassion according to the
abundance of his steadfast love; for
he does not willingly afflict or grieve
anyone"
(Lam 3:31-33).

</blockquote>

* * *

Bibliography

Maimonides, Moses. *Guide for the Perplexed*. Columbia, SC. No publisher
given, 2024.
The Jewish Study Bible, Tanakh Translation by the Jewish Publication Society,
Oxford University Press, 1995.

Note: Because the primary target audience for this book is Christian, a Christian Bible, (Renovaré Spiritual Formation Bible, New Revised Standard Version, HarperSanFrancisco:, 1989), was used as the main reference source. The book of Job, however, is a thoroughly Hebraic story but one that is theologically compatible with Christianity. That being the case, readers are encouraged to also refer to the Jewish version of the book of Job (The Jewish Study Bible, Tanakh Translation, Jewish Publication Society, Oxford University Press, 1995 is suggested). The Jewish rendering is much richer with more detailed footnotes, and the transliteration of select Old Testament Hebrew words offers another dimension to this fascinating story.

Suggested Group Discussion Questions

1. Do you think the book of Job is a factual or fictional account? Explain your reasoning.

2. What do you think was the book of Job author's purpose for writing it? (Consider the supposed post-exile time of composition.)

3. All of Job's family and servants were killed, except his wife. Why do you think she was spared?

4. How, if at all, is God's role in all of Job's misfortunes justified?

5. What did God mean when he condemns Job's friends saying they had "Not spoken of me what is right, as my servant Job has?"

6. Discuss the meaning behind Job's closing statement: "If I won, what have I won? If I lost, what have I lost? Who is this God?—Who am I?"

7. Find those contrasting sections in the book of Job where he reveals his actual fear of God and those sections where he is eager to confront God.

8. Have individuals role play reading from either the biblical book of Job or this book.

About the Author

Jack retired several years ago after a nearly forty-year career in healthcare as a psychiatric nurse and educator. The most profound part of his career was when he became involved in medical ethics, especially issues concerning end-of-life care. That involvement led him to the intersection of medical science and religion and prompted him to pursue an advanced degree in religion, leading to a Doctorate in Religious Studies. He has served on the ethics committee of two leading medical centers and his local hospice, where he is also a patient/family volunteer and grief counselor. He has published nursing and religious journal articles as well as two books. His current research interests are gospel origins and medieval theology and its centuries-long challenge to reconcile the philosophy of reason and the theology of faith. As an independent educator he has created lecture courses in Medieval Theology and also the relationship between early heresies and current Christian doctrines.

You can connect with me on:

🌐 https://jackcianciobooks.com

Also by Jack Ciancio

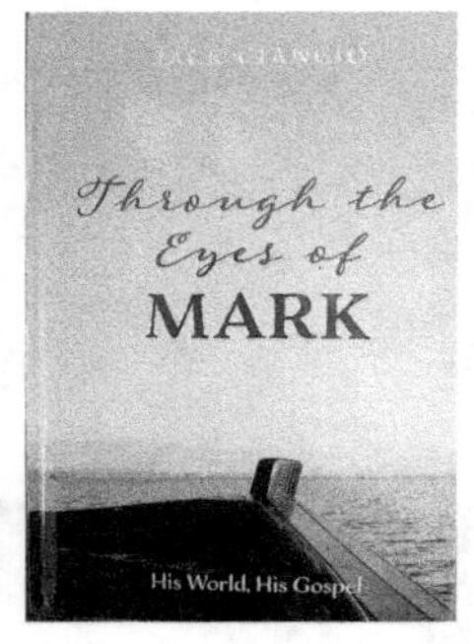

Through the Eyes of Mark: His World, His Gospel
(Wipf & Stock, 2021)

Mark's Gospel cannot be fully understood unless we recognize the spiritual needs, hopes, and fears of his first-century audience and emerging church. *Through the Eyes of Mark* immerses its readers in the realities of Mark's world. It presents the findings of dozens of the world's leading biblical and New Testament scholars and historians in an easy-to-understand format.

Through the Eyes of Mark is a must-read for students of religion, enlightening for general readers, and a fresh addition to the field of Markan studies.

Where Christ Presides: A Quaker Perspective on Moral Discernment
(Redemption Press, 2009)

Where Christ Presides presents a guide for readers to examine their own method of moral discernment within a Christ-centered continuum of moral development. Christians of all denominations, clergy, students and even nonbelievers will find this unique psycho-theological examination of Christian moral reasoning a useful guide for making ethical decisions.